The DRIFTWOOD Ball

For Lily, Kitty, Leo, Klara and Molly

– A TEMPLAR BOOK –

First published in the UK in 2014 by Templar Publishing,
an imprint of The Templar Company Limited,
Deepdene Lodge, Deepdene Avenue, Dorking, Surrey, RH5 4AT, UK
www.templarco.co.uk

Copyright © 2014 by Thomas Docherty

The illustrations were drawn with a dip pen and acrylic inks on
hot pressed watercolour paper and then painted in watercolour

First edition

ISBN 978-1-84877-709-5 (hardback)
ISBN 978-1-84877-988-4 (softback)

Designed by Nghiem Ta
Edited by Libby Hamilton

Printed in China

The DRIFTWOOD *Ball*

Thomas Docherty

templar publishing

In the sea by the forest there lived a family of otters. One particularly lively otter was called Celia.

and the otters didn't think much of the badgers.

And their food is bland and dull! -----

They're so stuffy and boring! -----

I think they seem quite sweet.

Only George and Celia felt differently.

You might have thought that the badgers and the otters had
nothing in common, but they did. They both loved to dance.

The badgers danced like this:

Jig –   jig –

And the otters danced like this:

Shimmy –   shimmy –

caper –

skip!

shimmy –

shoosh!

But George and Celia danced differently.

Jig –   jig –   caper...

Shimmy –   shimmy –   shimmy...

That's not how we badgers do things! ---

No, George love,
you've got it all wrong! ---

shoosh! went George.

Such a waste of talent! ---

Celia, pet, what do you
think you're doing? ---

skip! went Celia.

The only time the badgers and the otters got together was once a year at the Driftwood Ball.

On this special night a trophy was awarded to the best dancer.
And of course, everyone wanted to win it.

The badgers and otters practised their dance steps and moves every day in preparation for the big event.

Only George and Celia dreamed of being different.

The day before the Driftwood Ball, Celia felt fed up with shimmy this and shoosh that. She took one nimble jig and capered out of the sea.

Oh, hi! I'm Celia.

It was love

At the same time, George felt tired of all the **jigging** and **capering**. He *shooshed* out of the forest and down onto the beach.

Oh, hello! I'm George.

at first sight.

Shimmy-shimmy-skip! went Celia.

Jig-jig-caper-shoosh! went George.

First they danced
like this.

Then they danced
like that.

They danced backwards, upside down,

inside out

and sideways.

Over, under, in and out, and round
and round and round, until...

The next day was the Driftwood Ball itself. Badgers and otters from far and wide met on the beach and both sides began to dance.

The DRIF

The badgers danced with gusto:
jig-jig-caper-skip!

The otters danced with feeling:
shimmy-shimmy-shimmy-shoosh!

...OOD *Ball*

And no one noticed George and Celia, until suddenly...

...they started doing something different.
The band stopped. Everyone stared in amazement.
A badger and an otter, dancing together!

But Celia and George just kept on dancing.
The band started up again, and slowly some
of the badgers and otters began to clap.

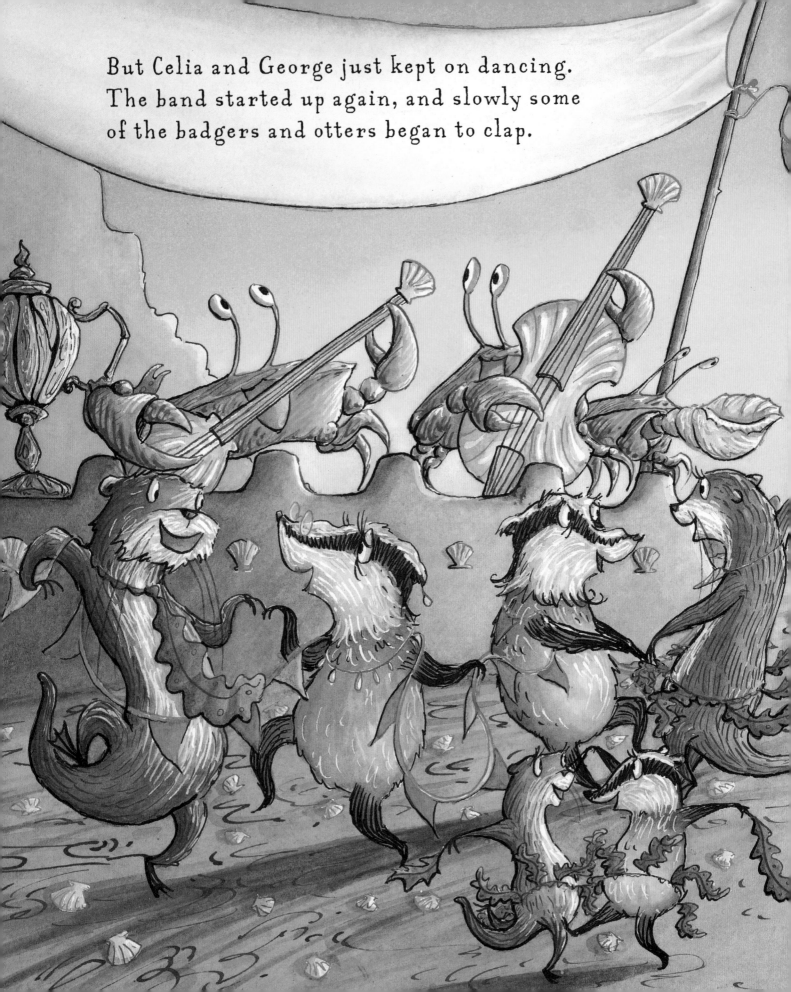

Soon they were all having so much fun that everyone
forgot their differences and began to dance together.
It was the best Driftwood Ball that anyone could remember.

When the time came to award the prizes,
it was obvious who the winners were.

But George and Celia were nowhere to be found.
They didn't care for prizes; they only cared for each other.

That night, the badgers and the otters realised
that they did quite like each other after all.

And George and Celia? They're still dancing...

... but always to their own tune.

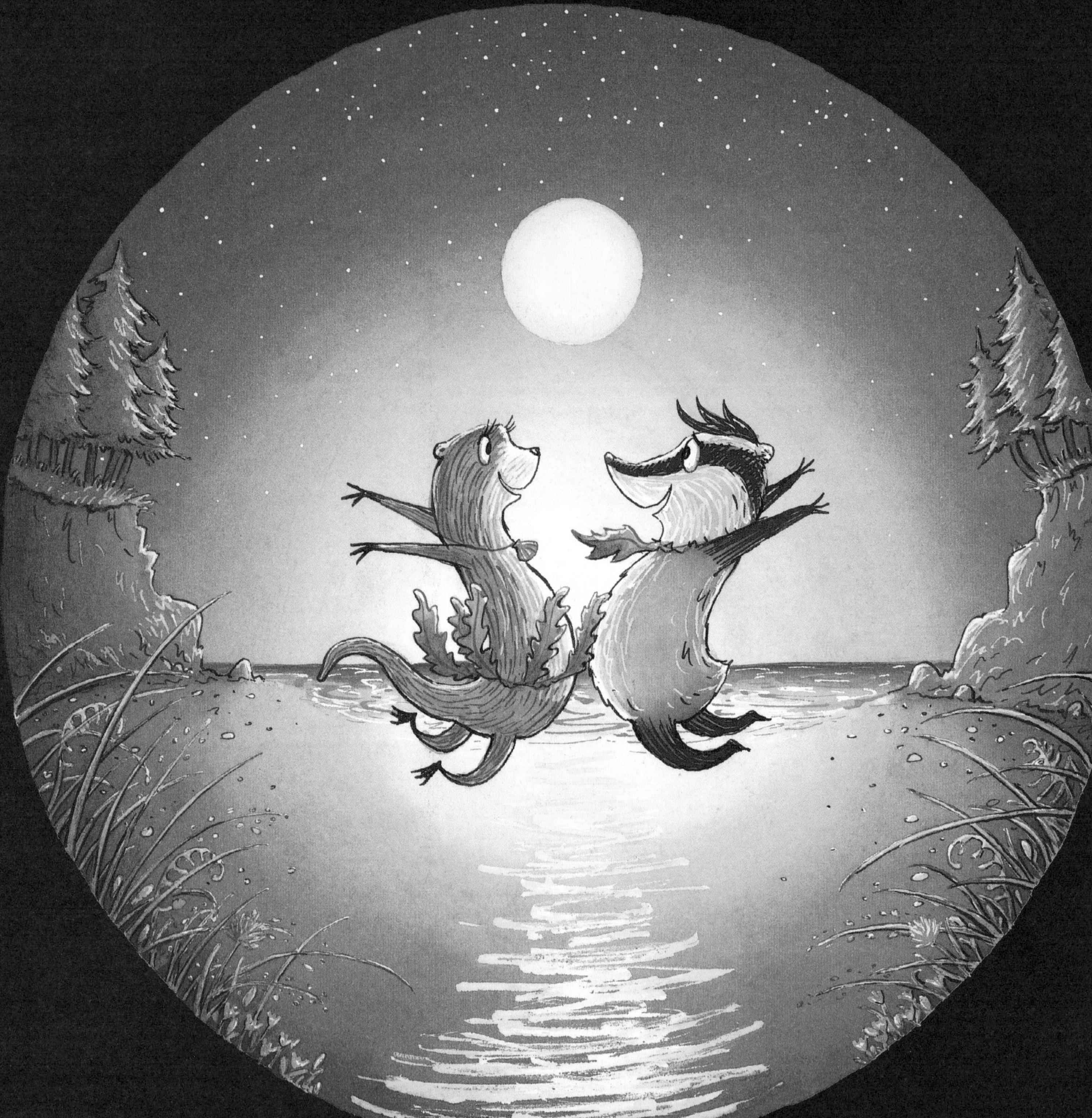

The End!